Walt Disney's

SCAMP

The Adventures of a Little Puppy

Told by Annie North Bedford
Pictures by the Walt Disney Studio
Adapted by Norm McGary and Joe Rinaldi

 A GOLDEN BOOK • NEW YORK

Library of Congress Control Number: 2004100454
ISBN: 0-7364-2311-7
www.goldenbooks.com
Printed in the United States of America
First Random House Edition 2004
10 9 8 7 6 5 4

Lady was the mother.
Tramp was the father.
Their puppies were the finest ever.
They were sure of that.

Three were as gentle and as pretty as their mother.

But the fourth little puppy—
"Where is that puppy? Where is that
Scamp?" they cried.

At mealtime three little gentle pretty puppies
would line up, waiting for their bowl.

But the fourth little puppy, that Scamp of a puppy, would rush in ahead of them all.

At playtime three little gentle pretty puppies
would play with their own puppy toys.

But the fourth little puppy, that Scamp of a puppy, would nibble at anything.

At bedtime three gentle pretty puppies would snuggle down to sleep.

But the fourth little puppy, that Scamp of
a puppy, chose that time to learn to howl,
loud and long.

One day the four little puppies started off for a picnic with nice puppy biscuits for lunch.

Three little puppies went straight to the
park and hunted for a shady spot.

But the fourth little puppy, that Scamp of
a puppy, went off on an adventure.

He found some new playmates.
Their game looked like fun.

But *Sss-ss-sst!* they didn't want Scamp to play.
So Scamp got out of there.

He found another playmate.
It was a busy gopher, digging as fast
as it could dig.

"Looks like fun," said Scamp. "How did you learn to do it?"

"By digging," Mr. Gopher said. So Scamp dug, too.

He dug and dug and dug.
And what do you think he found?
A big, juicy bone.
It was a great big bone for a small dog.

Scamp pulled at it.

He tugged and hauled.

He tugged that bone all the way down the
street to the park.

Just as Scamp got there, a big bad dog was saying, "Ha! I smell puppy biscuits."

So he sneaked up on those three little puppies and took their puppy-biscuit lunch.

Poor little puppies!
They were really very hungry. And they
felt very sad.

Just then, who should appear but the
fourth little puppy, that Scamp of a puppy,
tugging his great big bone!

"Hi, folks," he said. "Look what I found.
How about joining me?"
So they ate the big, juicy bone for lunch.
And they all had a fine time.

When picnic time was over those three pretty puppies all went happily home.

And the fourth little puppy, that Scamp of a puppy, walked proudly at the head of the line.